*This book is dedicated to all who have less,*
*but know they have more to give. – S.S.*

Published by Tuttle Publishing, an imprint of Periplus Editions (HK) Ltd.

**www.tuttlepublishing.com**

Copyright © 2012 Periplus Editions (HK) Ltd.

Library of Congress Cataloging in Process

ISBN 978-4-8053-1187-5

**Distributed by**

**North America, Latin America & Europe**
Tuttle Publishing
364 Innovation Drive
North Clarendon, VT 05759-9436 U.S.A.
Tel: 1 (802) 773-8930; Fax: 1 (802) 773-6993
info@tuttlepublishing.com
www.tuttlepublishing.com

**Japan**
Tuttle Publishing
Yaekari Building, 3rd Floor
5-4-12 Osaki; Shinagawa-ku
Tokyo 141 0032
Tel: (81) 3 5437-0171; Fax: (81) 3 5437-0755
sales@tuttle.co.jp
www.tuttle.co.jp

**Asia Pacific**
Berkeley Books Pte. Ltd.
61 Tai Seng Avenue, #02-12, Singapore 534167
Tel: (65) 6280-1330; Fax: (65) 6280-6290
inquiries@periplus.com.sg
www.periplus.com

First edition
17 16 15 14 13 12          10 9 8 7 6 5 4 3 2 1

Printed in Hong Kong          1110 CP

### THE TUTTLE STORY: "BOOKS TO SPAN THE EAST AND WEST"

Most people are very surprised to learn that the world's largest publisher of books on Asia had its beginnings in the tiny American state of Vermont. The company's founder, Charles E. Tuttle, belonged to a New England family steeped in publishing. And his first love was naturally books—especially old and rare editions.

Immediately after WW II, serving in Tokyo under General Douglas MacArthur, Tuttle was tasked with reviving the Japanese publishing industry, and founded the Charles E. Tuttle Publishing Company, which still thrives today as one of the world's leading independent publishers.

Though a westerner, Charles was hugely instrumental in bringing knowledge of Japan and Asia to a world hungry for information about the East. By the time of his death in 1993, Tuttle had published over 6,000 titles on Asian culture, history and art—a legacy honored by the Japanese emperor with the "Order of the Sacred Treasure," the highest tribute Japan can bestow upon a non-Japanese.

With a backlist of 1,500 books, Tuttle Publishing is as active today as at any time in its past—inspired by Charles' core mission to publish fine books to span the East and West and provide a greater understanding of each.

# YUKO-CHAN
## AND THE DARUMA DOLL

The Adventures of a Blind Japanese Girl Who Saves Her Village

Story and illustrations by
**SUNNY SEKI**

**TUTTLE** Publishing

Tokyo | Rutland, Vermont | Singapore

In Japan, there is an active volcano called Mount Asama. Two hundred years ago it erupted in flames. It then shot out ashes that covered the surrounding villages and damaged all the crops.

In the village of Takasaki, there lived an orphaned blind girl who stayed at the Daruma Temple. Her name was Yuko-chan, or Warm Water Girl, because she had such a warm, gentle personality.

ゆこちゃんとダルマさん
文と絵・サニー関

今から二百年前、浅間山がドドーンと大噴火をして、農作物に被害が出たときのお話です。高崎村のダルマ寺に、みなし子で目が見えない女の子がいました。気立てが優しく、お湯のように温かいというので、ゆこちゃんと呼ばれていました。

One night the head monk, Osho-san, met with village representatives to talk about ways to recover from the disaster. Yuko-chan overheard their worried voices and tried to calm them by serving them green tea.

ある晩、お寺で皆が「どうしたらば村を救えるだろう」と、話し合いました。その心配なようすに、ゆこちゃんはさっそくお茶を出しました。

The men could not think of a solution, so they began to read from their scriptures. Suddenly, a gust of wind blew out the candles, plunging the room into darkness. Everybody grew silent—except for Yuko-chan, who continued reciting the prayers, without skipping a word. "Why did you all stop?" she asked.

"We can't read in the dark!" they answered.

"Wow! You're handicapped aren't you?" she joked. They laughed, realizing that Yuko-chan had memorized all the words.

いい考えも出ないので、お経を読みをはじめると、ヒユーッと風がローソクを吹き消しました。ゆこちゃんだけの声になってしまい、彼女は「皆、どうして黙ったの?」と聞いたのです。「灯が消えて、お経が読めないんだ」との答えに、ゆこちゃんが、「じゃあ、皆は障害者じゃないの！」と言ったので大笑い。彼女はすべて、暗記していたのです。

The temple had a school where Osho-san taught children about Daruma-san, as well as how to read and write. Yuko-chan did not attend the school, but she always listened carefully to the lessons. She was eager to learn everything she could about Daruma-san.

お寺は、ダルマさんのことや読み書きを教えました、ゆこちゃんは生徒ではありませんが、熱心に聞き、いつも和尚さんにダルマさんの教えや姿を尋ねました。

One day when Osho-san had stepped out, the students jumped up to play with the musical instruments. Suddenly there was a shout: "Everyone stop! You are not in harmony!"

和尚さんの留守に、子ども達が楽器で騒いだことがあります。ゆこちゃんは、「ぜんぜん揃っていないねー」と声をかけずにはいられません。

It was Yuko-chan, who then began
beating the *taiko* in perfect rhythm.
"Dong chiki chin!  Dong chiki chin!"
she said, as she led the others.

Osho-san returned, and was
very impressed. "Wow!" he said to
himself, "This sounds like a concert!
Yuko-chan has talent! But I don't
want any unruly behavior in this
sacred place."

「こんな感じでいかなきゃ…」彼女が太鼓でリズムをとると、ドンチキチン、ドンチキチンと音楽らしくなり、演奏会にに変わりました。

　帰った和尚さんはビックリ。「ふーむ、ゆこちゃんは才能がある。楽しくて踊りたいくらいじゃ。しかし、こんな大切な場所で遊ばれては困る」と一喝。

"Enough!" he shouted. "These instruments are not toys. Let's get back to studying!"

Then Osho-san spoke very seriously:

"If we want to survive the loss of our crops, our village needs to find other ways to get money. In this difficult time, we must remember the teaching of our founder, Daruma-san.

He was a monk who preached all the way from India to China, meditating on Buddha's teachings for nine years! And though his arms and legs became numb, he still continued to spread his message:

'If you fall seven times, you must pick yourself up eight times! You need strong faith, and the belief that you can accomplish your goals!'"

These words inspired Yuko-chan.

「コラーッ！　お寺の楽器はオモチャではない。勉強へ戻れーっ！」

　和尚さんは心を込めて話しました。「村は災害で大変じゃ。農業の収入だけでは食べて行けん。こんな時こそダルマさんの教えを思い出そう。インドで生まれたダルマさんは中国へ行って仏教をひろめ、壁に向かい九年も座禅を続けたのじゃ。手足がしびれて抜け落ちても、ついに修行を終えたという。あきらめない勇気を「七転び八起き」、ぐらぐら揺れない気持ちを「不動心」と教えた。皆も見習わねばいけない」

　ゆこちゃんは、自分もダルマさんのようにがんばろうと思いました。

One night, Yuko-chan was startled awake by a suspicious sound. Shiba, her guide dog, heard it too.

"Shiba! I think someone is tipping over the donation box. Osho-san said that's what people do when they want to steal money!"

Shiba started to growl. "Shhh!" she whispered. "Let's catch the thief! I'll get your leash, and you stay quiet until I say to bark."

ある真夜中、ゴトゴトと怪しい音がします。愛犬シバも気づいて唸り出しました。これは和尚さんのいう賽銭泥棒に違いありません。

「シバ、吠えろ！と言うまで静かにしていてね。そーっと裏へ回って捕まえよう」

Yuko-chan tiptoed outside and shouted, "Don't move! Or I'll release the dog!" Shiba started to bark loudly.

In the moonlight a young man stood frozen—with a handful of coins.

"Please don't let your dog attack me!" He cried. "My father is sick and I need to buy him some medicine!"

Yuko-chan felt sorry for him. "Okay. But you had better leave before Osho-san gets here!"

Osho-san arrived in time to see the man running away. "I wish our temple could do more to help those people," he sighed.

「ちょっとでも動くと飛びかからせるよっ！」
泥棒の後から、ゆこちゃんは大声を浴びせました。シバは噛みつきそうに吠えます。

賽銭箱からお金を拾っていた青年は驚いて動けません。彼は「犬をけしかけないで！

父が病気で、薬を買うお金が要るんだ」と、必死に頼みました。ゆこちゃんはかわいそうになり、

「和尚さんが来るまでに、要るだけ取って逃げなさい」と言ったのです。

Osho-san began visiting villagers to collect extra food for people in need. Yuko-chan often tagged along with Shiba at her side.

At one of the houses she recognized a familiar voice talking with Osho-san—It was the thief!

"My father was sick, but I was able to buy some good medicine, and now he is feeling better!"

"I'm glad to hear that," said Osho-san. Yuko-chan was relieved that this young man, named Kenta, had used the money from the temple honestly. She didn't tell Osho-san that Kenta had stolen it.

和尚さんは困っている人に、食べ物を届けはじめたので、ゆこちゃんも手伝います。ある家で青年の声に聞き覚えがありました。「ご心配かけましたが、良い薬が買えたので父の病気は治りかけています」「それはよかった。健太、お大事にな」と話しているのを聞いて、ゆこちゃんはうれしく思ったのです。ですから泥棒のことは言いませんでした。

One day Osho-san was away, and it was up to Yuko-chan and Shiba to deliver the food alone. After stopping at Kenta's house, they turned back toward the temple.

As they traveled it started to snow, and Yuko-chan became disoriented by the weather. She accidentally took a wrong path—one that led into the mountains!

隣り村に出かけた和尚さんに替わり、ゆこちゃんが配達した日のことです。彼女もシバも道は覚えていて、一番遠くの健太の家までゆくと、彼の父は、かなり良くなっていました。ところが、帰りは雪が降りだし、間違って山へ入ってしまったのです。

"Shiba, I think we're lost!" No sooner had Yuko-chan spoken these words than she stumbled, and they both tumbled over a cliff!

迷ったので戻ろうとしたゆこちゃんは、つまずいたとたん、
シバと崖から落ち、アッと気が付くと地面が無いではありませんか！

Luckily, Yuko-chan landed on her soft backpack, and Shiba plopped onto the powdery snow.

"Help! Help!" Yuko-chan called, but there was no response. Feeling thirsty, she reached around for her tea gourd, but it kept dropping from her shivering fingers. Suddenly, Yuko-chan noticed something very unusual.

"Shiba! This is mysterious. Every time I drop the gourd, it rolls upside down ... and then ... koro-koro-rin! ... it comes back up again!"

「ドサーン！」背負ったカゴがクッションになったので助かりました。大声で人を呼びましたが誰も通りません。のどが枯れ、水をいれた瓢箪を探しましたが、カゴからはずれてしまったようです。やっと見つけた瓢箪は、スルリとかじかんだ手から抜け、コロ、コロ、コロリ〜ン！と転んだ先で立ち上がりました。また、転がしても必ず、まっすぐ立つので不思議です。

Yuko-chan was so fascinated that she forgot they were lost. "Look! The frozen tea in the bottom keeps the gourd upright! Even though it falls, it gets up again—just like Daruma-san's teaching! And the shape is just like his: no arms and no legs!"

Then she had a bright idea. "What if we made these at the temple, and called them 'Daruma Dolls'? Could we sell them and save our village?"

It was an exciting idea, but she was really starting to feel cold. So Yuko-chan cuddled up with Shiba under a tree. As she dozed off, she felt like she heard a distant voice calling her name.

おもしろくなったゆこちゃんは、心細さも忘れて繰り返しました。コロ、コロ、コロリ～ン！「中の水が凍って、おもりになっているんだ。転んでも起きるなんてダルマさんみたい。手も足も無いし・・・」と笑ったとき、「この人形をお寺で売ったら、村はお金持ちにならないかしら？」と考えついたのです。

「どうやって作ったら…」と思っているうちに寒くなり、木の根元でシバと抱きあいました。眠りそうになったとき、誰かが自分を呼んだようです。

"Yuko-chan, are you there?"
It was Kenta, who had gone
searching for them.

　"Arf! Arf!" answered Shiba.
Yuko-chan was so relieved.

　"Oh, Kenta! Thank you for finding us.
We are safe, but we need help!"

「おーい、ゆこちゃん。
大丈夫かーい？」健太の声に、
まずシバが「ウォーン！」と答えました。
雪になったので、傘を持ち足跡を追ってきて
草履を見つけたのです。「私もシバも大丈夫。
でも助けがいるわ。健太、ありがとぉー！」

They returned to Kenta's house for a hearty dinner. Yuko-chan enthusiastically explained her idea and asked for advice. "You should use bamboo," Kenta's father suggested. Kenta showed her how to weave the stems together.

Kenta then lowered his head and quietly said, "I need to apologize to you and the temple. What I did was…" Yuko-chan interrupted. "We can't dwell on what's been done in the past, Kenta. We have to think about how we can make our future better!" Kenta's eyes brightened. "I will be happy to help your project by donating bamboo to the temple!"

暖かい夕食のあと、ゆこちゃんがダルマ人形のアイデアを話すと、健太の父は「竹ヒゴで形を作りなさい」と言い、健太は編み方を教えてくれました。

そして小声で、「ぼくは、君とお寺に謝らなければいけないんだ。じつは…」と言い出したので、ゆこちゃんは、「済んだことよりも、これからやれる良いことがたくさんあるよね」と答えました。「そうだ。竹ヒゴだったらいくらでも上げるよ！」と、健太はうれしそうに目を輝かせたのです。

Yuko-chan returned home and started to test many ideas. She finally decided to place a rock in the bottom, add a paper covering, and then paint the entire doll. This dream had to come true!

帰ってから、ゆこちゃんは竹に紙を貼って、何回も転がしてみました。シバも見守っています。石のおもりの加減が難しいのですが、この人形に村を救ってもらおうと、一生懸命です。

Finally the doll was ready to be presented to Osho-san.
   When the children saw it, they began to laugh, "Look at that funny ball!"
Yuko-chan ignored them as she approached Osho-san.

ついにダルマ人形を和尚さんに見せることにしました。「あれっ、ゆこちゃんが変なものを持ってきたぞ！」と子どもたちが、からかっても彼女は真剣でした。

Yuko-chan proclaimed, "I believe that Daruma-san will save our village!"

Osho-san replied, "Yuko-chan, I only wish it were that simple."

"But that is why I have made this doll. It honors Daruma-san's words: if you fall down seven times, you should get up eight times! I hope we can sell these to save our village."

The children continued teasing:

"What's that? A broken ball is Daruma-san? Ha ha! Whoever heard of that?" However, Osho-san was intrigued. "Let me see how it works." He released the doll on the ground. It rolled over and over … and then it stood upright! At first the children grew silent, but then they suddenly started to cheer.

和尚さん、私はダルマさんに村を救ってもらいたいと思います」「その通りだけども、ゆこちゃん、それがむずかしいのじゃ」和尚さんは訳がわかりません。

「これは七転び八起きのダルマさん人形です。見て教えがわかり、売れたら皆が助かるのではと…」後は、子どもたちの「なーんだ、こわれた毬みたいのがダルマさんだって… わっはっは」という笑い声で聞こえません。

「じゃ、その人形を転がしてみよう」ということになりました。コロ、コロ、コロリ～ン！ ダルマ人形がスックと立つと、皆の呼吸が止まり続いて歓声が上がりました。

"This is wonderful! We will sell these at the Spring Festival!" Osho-san said as he tested the doll again and again. Then he noticed that Yuko-chan had left the doll's eyes blank. "We will honor this by suggesting that people darken the left pupil when they make a wish, and the right pupil when the wish comes true. We are going to be busy!" Yuko-chan was overjoyed.

何回か試した和尚さんは「これは良い。春祭りに売り出そう。人形に目玉がないのを利用して、目的を決めたら左目を、成しとげたら右目を入れる。ゆこちゃんの思いつきを大切に、白い目から始めよう。さあ、皆で作るのじゃ、忙しくなるぞ！」と大満足です。

The villagers loved the idea, and rushed to begin making their own dolls. Somehow the dolls always seemed to look a little bit like the people who had made them!

村人はゆこちゃんから作り方を聞くと、張り切って取りかかりました。人形は何となく作る人に似てくるようです。

The Spring Festival came, and people flocked from far and wide to buy the clever Daruma dolls. Yuko-chan beat the *taiko*, and Kenta played his flute. The joyful people could not help but dance to the catchy rhythm of the music.

From that day forward, the village was saved. Even today the Daruma dolls of Takasaki are the most famous in all of Japan.

春祭りには遠くの町や村から人が来て、ダルマ人形はどんどん売れました。ゆこちゃんの太鼓と健太の笛もピタリとあって、聞けば踊らずにはいられません。こうして村は救われ、高崎のダルマ人形は日本中で有名になりました。

Some time later Yuko-chan left the village to study under a famous *taiko* teacher. Kenta, whose father was now healthy, escorted her. As they left the village, he noticed the smoke rising from Mount Asama.

"Yuko-chan, it's the shape of a Daruma doll!" She smiled and said. "Just think. If the volcano had not erupted, there would never have been Daruma dolls. What started as a disaster has turned into a golden opportunity for everyone!"

やがて、ゆこちゃんは太鼓の勉強のため村を出ることになり、父親が直った健太が付き添って行きます。峠に立つと浅間山が見えました。「ダルマさんみたいな形の煙が上がっているよ。ゆこちゃん」健太が声をかけると、彼女は「もし、噴火しなかったら、ダルマさん人形も生まれなかった。"災いを転じて福となす"って難しそうだけれど、やろうと思えばできるんだよね」と答えたということです。おしまーい。

# Cultural Notes

**Daruma—Father of Zen Buddhism** Daruma was an Indian monk who lived in the early sixth century. He traveled to China to establish his teachings, which became known in Japan as Zen Buddhism. After meditating for nine years in a cave near the Shorinji Temple in China, he reached a pure state of thought—enlightenment, or *satori*. For that entire time he had been sitting in *zazen*, in which both legs are crossed close to the body and the arms do not move. According to legend, he was in this position for so long that all four of his limbs became numb, until they shriveled, and finally fell off!

**A Conversation with the Chinese King** The teaching of Daruma can be summarized in this famous conversation: A king, who had built many temples, approached Daruma. Expecting praise, he asked, "What merit have I earned by all that I have contributed?" To his dismay, Daruma replied, "None." Then the king asked, "What is the meaning of your teachings?" Daruma replied, "Only emptiness … nothing sacred." Finally, the king asked, "Who are you?" The response was, "I don't know." This conversation is the basis of all Zen teaching.

**Daruma Doll** These dolls are shaped like Daruma himself, seated in *zazen*. He is meditating, and thus clearing his mind to become totally free. They are painted as if they are wearing a red robe. When tipped over, they always return to an upright position, symbolizing success as one overcomes misfortune or adversity. It is customary to make a wish, and then paint the left eye. When the wish comes true, the right eye is painted. Therefore, Daruma dolls are symbols of goal setting, and they are often gifts of encouragement.

**Daruma Doll Festival** This celebration is held every year at Shorinzan Temple, or "Daruma-dera," near the city of Takasaki, in Gunma-ken near Tokyo. This city boasts that more than 400,000 people buy their Daruma dolls every year. In fact, Takasaki produces eighty percent of all Daruma dolls made in Japan.

**Daruma Games** Many children's activities mention Daruma. The winter snowman is called *yukidaruma*, or "snow Daruma." *Daruma otoshi* is a traditional toy consisting of a Daruma doll that has been cut and stacked into five horizontal slices; then a small hammer is used to knock away each piece from bottom to the top, without letting any pieces fall. Finally, *darumasan ga koronda* is a playful way of counting, in ten syllables: だるまさんがころんだ。

**Gourds** Gourds have been useful all over the world, and in Japan they were traditionally used to hold saké or any other liquid. Hideyoshi, who united Japan before 1600, used the gourd in war as a symbol of good luck.